The Lightkeeper's Key

Angeli Perrow

To Orion —
A good book is a treasure.
Enjoy the mystery!

Your art teacher —
Angeli Perrow
2010

ISBN: 1-4392-5581-4
ISBN-13: 9781439255810
Library of Congress Control Number: 2009908834

To order additional copies, please contact us.
BookSurge
www.booksurge.com
1-866-308-6235
orders@booksurge.com

Dedication

For Gabriel, my son-shine

Chapter 1: The Ghost of the Tower

Far out to sea, the mournful moan of a foghorn sounded. The circling beam of the lighthouse stabbed the night sky over and over. The air was damp and fingers of mist clawed at the moon.

They stood on the rocky shore just below the lighthouse.

"I bet you never saw a sight like this in Nevada," Mandy said.

Nick craned his neck to gaze up at the tower. "It's kind of creepy."

The white buildings seemed to glow with an eerie light.

"Hey, did you see something move?" he whispered, pointing at the keeper's house. "Over there!"

In a slow, spooky voice Mandy announced, "It's—the—ghost."

The boy gulped. "The *g-ghost?*"

"The ghost of old Captain Kimball, first keeper of Dyer Point Light. On foggy nights he wanders 'round the lighthouse, looking for the key."

"K-key?" stuttered Nick. "The k-key to what?"

Careful, Mandy thought. She did not want to tell her cousin about the key. He looks like a gawky scarecrow, she thought—black hair sticking up like straw, skinny arms dangling. "Nobody knows," she intoned in her best graveyard voice. "Keepers of the lighthouse after him found mysterious footprints on the walkway on nights like this. The locked door of the tower would be open."

Nick gaped at her. "How did the Captain die?" he asked in a hoarse voice.

"They say he was found at the base of the tower one morning with dead birds all around him." She paused for effect. "*He* was dead, too."

"Wh-what happened?"

"The birds smashed against the glass of the lantern room. The Captain climbed out on the catwalk to help the birds that were still alive. Maybe another bird flew in and knocked him over, maybe he was startled, maybe he slipped. No one knows for sure. But he fell from the tower to the rocks below. Maybe right where we're standing." Mandy shivered. She was even scaring herself.

Nick touched her arm. His upturned face was frozen in a mask of fear. Before she could turn her head, the silence was shattered by the piercing cry of the lighthouse foghorn. Nick screamed. Slipping and sliding like a demented seal, he floundered across the seaweed-covered rocks and stumbled onto the path.

What had he seen? Mandy looked up at the lighthouse, but it had been swallowed by the fog.

Chapter 2: The Mysterious Key

"Tell me about the key, Papa Gene," Mandy said, taking it off the nail where it always hung in his workshop.

"Can you keep a secret?"

"Of course I can," Mandy replied, leaning closer to hear her grandfather's hushed voice.

"A century ago, out near Little Crumple, something terrible happened. There was a December gale a-blowin' fierce. A schooner, bound for Boston with a load of lumber, struck the ledge. Captain Isaiah Kimball, first keeper of Dyer Point Light, set out in the skiff to try and rescue the crew. His wife begged him not to go, but he had to do his duty. As he battled the wind and waves, she lit a bonfire on the shore and prayed for his safe return. Well, he returned later that night, but not in the skiff. He washed up on the shore, battered and bruised, nearly dead. And he wasn't the same man."

Hanging on every word, Mandy whispered, "What do you mean, Papa Gene?"

"The Captain's mind was gone, poor man. Like a ship without a rudder. Like a lantern with the light snuffed out. Couldn't speak. Just stared, empty-eyed, like no one was home. People figured he'd seen something too horrible for his mind to bear."

Mandy's eyes widened. "What could do *that* to a person?"

"No one knows for sure. There was terrible suffering that night. Trying to stay above the pounding waves, the sailors clung to the ship's rigging, crying out for help, and there they froze."

Mandy squeezed her eyes tight, trying to shut out the awful picture in her mind of the frozen men hanging from the ropes. And then she remembered the key. "What about the key, Papa Gene?"

"The key was in the Captain's pocket when he washed up on the beach. His wife had never seen it before. She hung it on a nail in the lighthouse and there it stayed for nigh on eighty years. One night I was playing checkers with Ben Blake, the last keeper, and he told me the story. Said I could have the key, if I wanted."

"Did you ever look on the island?" Mandy had asked. "Maybe there was a treasure." Little

Crumple was only a stone's throw from the ledge where the ship sank.

"Sure did," he replied. "Never found a thing. But I feel it in my bones that the answer to the mystery is there somewhere on Little Crumple."

Mandy had studied the key with growing excitement. It was important or the Captain wouldn't have put it in his pocket. There was no doubt in her mind—it had to be the key to a treasure box of some kind.

Now, a year later, it was time. Time to search for the treasure. Her father had promised that when she turned ten she would be old enough to row *Raven* out to Little Crumple by herself. But there was a complication. Her mind flashed back to the moment this afternoon when she had heard the bad news.

"You've got to be kidding," Mandy said. "Nick is coming for the summer—the *whole* summer?" She tugged on her short brown hair and wrinkled her freckled nose. Her voice rose to a squeak. "My vacation is...is...*ruined*!"

"Now, Mandy, calm down," her mother said. "Think of your poor cousin. His father has lost his job. The family can't afford to go anywhere or do anything. Your father and I thought it would be a nice break for Nick to come to Maine and enjoy himself."

Mandy blinked back tears of outrage. "Enjoy himself!" she wailed. "What about *me*? How can I enjoy myself if I have to babysit that big over-grown...clumsy klutz? When Nick was here last summer, he trampled the blueberry bushes and kicked over the pail. It took *me* forever to pick up all the berries. He dropped the fishing pole off the dock and *I* had to dive in and find it because *he* can't swim. And at Papa Gene's funeral, he kept sneezing and coughing. He spoils everything!"

"Mandy Lynn Morrison, that's enough," her mother warned in her no-nonsense voice. "Nick has allergies. That's not his fault. And he's going through an awkward stage, all arms and legs. That happens to boys when they're twelve or so. Any-way, I promised my sister we would help out in whatever way we can. And so we will."

Mandy trudged upstairs to her room as, in her mind's eye, the whole vacation evaporated into smoke. The precious summer days of fishing, berry-picking, exploring—pouf! Her tenth sum-mer, the summer of looking for the treasure.

From under her bed, she pulled out the wood-en box given to her by Papa Gene. She moved her fingers over the scene he had carved on the lid—

a dolphin arcing over the ocean waves—and she could almost hear her grandfather's voice.

"You can storm against what life dishes out to you," he used to tell her, "but it only whips up a northeaster in here." He would tap his heart. "Or you can batten down the hatches and ride out the storm—see where the sea takes you." Mandy didn't always understand—Papa Gene's days of fishing the Grand Banks had salted his thoughts with sea talk. But his quiet words always seemed to calm her. How she missed him. Last August when he died was the saddest day of her life. It left this big empty hole in her heart.

Mandy opened the lid of the box. She sifted through the shells and sea glass and lifted out the tarnished old key. It fit perfectly into the palm of her hand. It was shaped like a skeleton key, but smaller, and was embellished with odd figures and designs like ancient hieroglyphs. It was the key from the old lightkeeper's pocket. The key from her grandfather's workshop. Now it was hers. And this summer she was determined to find the trea-sure—*if* she could keep her cousin Nick out of the way long enough.

Chapter 3: Echoes From the Past

Nick, pale and quiet, sat at the kitchen table eating cereal. Mrs. Morrison was cooking poached eggs on the stove. She had the radio tuned to an oldies station and was singing along to a Beatles song.

"I'll just have cereal, Mom," Mandy announced as she breezed into the room and perched on a stool across from her cousin.

"Well, good morning to you, too," her mother replied. She spooned more water over the eggs. "Nick's feeling a little under the weather this morning." She added, jokingly, "He looks like he's seen a ghost."

Startled, Mandy glanced at Nick, just in time to see an odd expression flash across his face. "Okay, Nick, 'fess up," she whispered behind the cereal box. "What did you see at the lighthouse last night?"

Her cousin just stared into his bowl and kept on munching.

Mandy kicked him under the table. "Nick," she hissed. "*Did* you see the ghost?"

He glared at her. "I saw *something*. I don't know *what* it was." Abruptly, he stood up, overturning the stool. It clattered on the tile floor. "Sorry, Aunt Susan," he mumbled to Mandy's mother. "I'm not feeling very well." He lurched from the room.

Mrs. Morrison sighed. "Poor boy. I think he's homesick. Mandy, you should do something today to get his mind off it."

"I'll do my best," Mandy said. She doubted Nick's mind was on home right now. But why was he acting so weird? You would think if he saw something scary, he would want to talk about it. *She* sure wanted to talk about it. Mandy had been at Dyer Point Light *hundreds* of times and had never seen a ghostly figure flitting about. She would pry it out of him somehow.

Later in the morning, Mandy tapped on the guest room door. "Come on, Nick," she called. "Let's go get ice cream. Sylvester's has the best caramel fudge swirl in the world!" She figured he wouldn't be able to resist that.

The door opened a crack. "Okay," he said. "Just hold on a minute." Mandy pushed the door open a little wider with her foot. Nick had a book in his hand—her father's faded volume of *The*

History of Dyer Cove. Why is he reading that boring old book? Mandy wondered. She had never thought of Nick as much of a reader unless it was comic books.

At the take-out, they ordered cones and sat on the edge of the town wharf, dangling their feet above the deep green water. Between licks of her ice cream, Mandy asked, "So, Nick, have you read any good books lately?"

"As a matter-of-fact, I've been reading about the lighthouse," he replied. "I found out about the birds. It turns out that in certain weather conditions, the light in the tower attracted them like a magnet. They would smash into the glass and fall to the ground, stunned. One time a big duck hurtled in and broke the window in the lantern room. The keeper went to investigate, found the dead duck, and served it up for Thanksgiving dinner the next day."

Mandy was listening so intently that she forgot to eat her ice cream. Fudge sauce dripped on her hand.

"I found out something else, too," Nick continued. "About Captain Kimball, the first keeper."

"What?" Mandy asked.

"He and his wife had a child that got very sick and died. A baby girl. He built a tiny coffin and buried her behind the lighthouse." Nick paused and swallowed hard. "That's what I saw last night."

Mandy stared at him, eyes wide. "What do you mean? You saw what?"

"The Captain carrying the coffin. With his wife walking behind. You know, the funeral procession. Or at least that's what it looked like before they disappeared in the fog."

Chapter 4: In the Shadows

"We have to go back," Mandy said when she had recovered from the shock of Nick's words.

"No way." Nick shook his head. "Wild horses couldn't drag me back there."

"Are you chicken?"

"No, just smart. Dabbling in the spirit world can be dangerous. Count me out."

"Big chicken," she whispered to herself. This was one time when she would have been glad of his company. Aloud, she said, "Well, I'll go alone then. . . as soon as it's dark."

"I'll wait for you on the path," he offered.

"Gee, thanks," she murmured. "If I'm not back in an hour, you can call in the Marines!"

After dinner that evening, Mandy and Nick started down the path to the lighthouse. Tree branches met overhead, creating a gloomy tunnel. The woodsy fragrance of the fir needles underfoot mixed with the salty tang of the sea air. Mandy breathed in deeply. This time she had brought a flashlight, even though the sky was clear and the moon was rising. Carrying the light made her feel a little braver. At the shortcut, they stopped.

"Are you sure you want to do this?" Nick asked, as he kicked at a rock on the path.

"I *have* to find out what's going on," Mandy replied. "Are you sure you don't want to come?" She crossed her fingers, hoping he would change his mind.

Nick looked at his feet. "I'm sure."

"Okay then." Mandy's heart was pounding. She sucked in a big breath and, clutching the flashlight, started across the rocky cove. The tide was out and the fishy smell of wet seaweed surrounded her. The flashlight beam flickered over the uneven surface, helping her to find her way across the moonscape of menacing black shapes. Huge boulders brushed with silvery light loomed in the darkness like beached whales. The surf shushed in the distance. Below the lighthouse she stopped and glanced up. Not a ghost in sight.

The lighthouse, gleaming white in the moonlight, looked solid and strong. Every eight seconds its beam flashed out over the dark water, warning ships away from the dangerous rocks. Its familiar presence gave her courage to go on.

Mandy drew in another breath and climbed the faint trail to the base of the tower. According to Papa Gene, no one had lived in the lighthouse for thirty years. The light was automatic now and didn't need a keeper. The buildings were locked with sturdy padlocks, but Mandy had found her own way in.

Holding the flashlight in front of her, she removed a loose section of lattice and crawled underneath the front porch of the keeper's house. The light reflected off the grimy glass of a basement window. She found the stick she used to prop open the window, put it in place, and slithered through the opening feet first, landing on a chair she had set there on a past visit. She jumped down onto the dirt floor.

This was her least favorite part of the lighthouse, the cellar under the keeper's house. It was cold and musty, draped with spider webs, and she could hear the sound of water dripping. It was just the way she imagined a medieval dungeon to be, with its prisoners groaning in agony.

She had never been here at night before. She stood rooted to the spot, moving the flashlight over the dusty objects in front of her—an old sofa, a pile of wooden crates, a broken hat rack. They threw strange shadows on the wall, tall looming shapes like monsters searching for victims.

"Stop it," Mandy said to herself. Something scurried over her foot. At the same time, someone—or some*thing*—called her name. It was too much. Mandy scrambled up onto the chair and through the window, knocking away the stick. The window dropped like a guillotine, pinning her foot. In panic, she pulled and pulled. Her foot wedged tighter. "Help!" she squawked.

"Mandy, where are you?"

Her name again, but this time she recognized the voice.

"Nick, under the porch!"

Her cousin found the spot where she had removed the lattice and peered in. She turned the flashlight on his face and he cringed.

"Come on, you've got to get out of there!" he said. "They're coming."

"I can't! My foot is stuck!" she cried. "Help me!"

Nick slid into the dark, dusty space. He took the flashlight from Mandy and aimed it at her foot. In a matter of seconds, he had the window up and her foot was free.

She headed for the opening, but Nick grabbed her arm to stop her. "Wait!" he whispered. "They're here." He snapped off the light.

Mandy wriggled in his grasp. Loud creaks came from the porch floor boards over their heads. She stopped struggling. "Who is it?" she asked, her eyes wide.

Nick put a finger to his lips to silence her. "The ghosts."

Chapter 5: Footsteps in the Night

"This place gives me the creeps," a woman's voice said in a low voice.

"Don't worry, Suze, it's perfect," replied a man. "Isolated. No one ever comes here. And it stays locked. Except to me, of course."

"That was smart of you to replace the padlock with one of your own. From the outside, everything looks the same."

"Yeah. It will fool the occasional snoopy tourist and the local yokels, too."

Under the porch, Mandy and Nick listened. The sound of loud footsteps entering the house and the door opening and closing, eased the tension. Mandy let out her breath in a relieved 'whoosh'.

"Ghosts, huh?" she hissed. "Sure sounds like human beings to me."

"Well, uh. . ."

"Never mind. I wonder what these people are up to," she whispered.

"Must be squatters."

"What's that?"

"People who move into an empty place without permission. We get them out West all the time. Maybe we should tell your parents."

Mandy was quiet for a moment. There was a scraping sound and a thump from inside. "No, not yet. They're up to something. And I want to find out what it is."

"Sh-h-h, they're coming!"

They heard the door opening and closing and the creak of the porch floorboards. The lock clicked shut.

"There. We're as ready as we'll ever be," the male voice announced. "A perfect plan. We'll be set for life."

Mandy *had* to get a look at them. She started crawling toward the opening.

"No, Mandy!" Nick whispered. He grabbed at her foot to stop her.

"Hey, did you hear something?" the man exclaimed. He stopped right above where the children crouched. "I could have sworn. . ."

"Mike, this place isn't haunted, is it?" came Suze's voice in a high-pitched quiver.

Maybe it was nerves or maybe it was the thought of being mistaken for ghosts by the 'ghosts', but Mandy had to clasp her hand over her mouth to stifle a laugh. The sound came out as a muffled snort.

"Mike, let's get out of here," the woman said.

"Wait a minute," Mike said. "I did hear something . . . under the porch." He stomped hard, making Nick and Mandy jump.

"Better not do that," the woman warned. "It might be a skunk."

"Yeah, . . . you're right. Let's go."

The couple hurried off down the path. Mandy kicked Nick's hand away and dived toward the opening. In the moonlight, she caught a glimpse of the pair before they disappeared into the woods, but she could not see their faces.

"Come on, Nick, let's follow them," she urged, as her cousin crawled out from under the porch. She was already racing toward the path.

"Wait, Mandy," Nick called. "Slow down." He brushed dirt off his tee-shirt and jeans and glanced around. He shivered and hurried after Mandy. He stumbled down the trail, his feet catching on roots while branches grabbed at him like skeleton hands. The moonlight did not penetrate the gloom of the forest. "Why didn't I bring a flashlight?" Nick moaned to himself.

Suddenly, a shape, darker than the trees, rose up in front of him. His eyes widened in horror. He tried to stop himself, but just then his foot caught on a root and he sprawled into the dark form. *Thud.* It beat at him with bony hands like hammers. It scratched at his face with nails like daggers. He squealed in terror.

"Nick! You oaf!" Mandy's voice hissed. "Get off me!"

Nick pulled away from her and placed a hand over his thumping heart. "Good grief!" he murmured. "What are you doing crouching in the middle of the path? You nearly gave me a heart attack."

"I was listening."

"To what?"

"The squatters, or whoever they are," Mandy said. "They were talking about tomorrow. And money. Something's going to happen tomorrow."

"Hey, maybe they're planning to rob a bank. We should tell the police."

"Nick, we don't know who they are. And we can't even describe what they look like. . . since I got interrupted in my spying."

"Uh, sorry. . ." Nick mumbled.

Mandy knew it was impossible to follow the couple now. With Nick thrashing through the woods, they would be heard a mile away. And she didn't dare turn on the flashlight to help them see their way. She sighed. "We might as well head home. . . and see what tomorrow brings."

Chapter 6: Treasure in the Attic

"Do you kids have any plans for today?" Mrs. Morrison asked at breakfast. She smoothed cream cheese on a toasted bagel and held it in the air, her eyebrows raised.

Mandy knew that look. It meant her mother had plans for them. There were a million things she'd *like* to do. Check out the wild strawberries over in Turner's field. Fish for mackerel off the dock. Row out to Little Crumple. She eyed Nick, who was eating his Cheerios with gusto this morning. Couldn't go anywhere with him around. Most of all, she was itching to sneak back to the lighthouse and see what the squatters had carried in there last night. The need to know was burning a hole in her brain. It was useless, though, to make excuses to her mother. Mandy sighed. "No, nothing special planned."

"Good," her mother said. "I need your help. There are ten boxes in the attic you can load into the van. Then you can ride with me down to Union Hall. The festival committee is setting up for the

Flash for the Fourth Flea Market. The more we sell, the better the fireworks display will be on the 4th of July."

Nick carried his empty bowl to the sink. "Sure, Aunt Susan. These muscles could use a workout." He flexed a bicep.

Mandy almost choked on a banana slice. That's for sure, she thought. His muscle looked like a deflated balloon.

"Are you all right, Dear?" her mother asked with concern.

"Yeah, fine." Mandy cleared her throat. "When do we start?"

"The sooner, the better. I'll back the van up to the door."

Mandy and Nick climbed the narrow wooden stairs to the attic. Dust motes floated in the sunbeams shining through the window. This was Mandy's favorite place on a rainy day. Trunks and boxes lined the walls, filled with interesting things that had belonged to her grandparents. She barely remembered her grandmother. Mandy had been only five when Nana died. She did remember, though, soft warm hugs and the scent of lilacs. And she remembered Papa Gene's tears. It had frightened her to see her grandfather crying.

Now she understood how it felt to lose someone you love. A loud sneeze interrupted her thoughts.

"It sure is dusty up here," Nick said. "I'm al— ler- ler- gic. . . ah—*choo*...to dust."

More like allergic to work, Mandy thought. "Well, wait at the bottom of the stairs," she suggested, "and I'll bring the boxes down to you." She would rather be alone in the attic anyway.

Nick clomped down the stairs with the first box.

Out of curiosity, Mandy lifted the lid of another box. What was her mother giving away? Ten boxes was a lot of stuff. She rummaged through the contents—an old coffee pot, crocheted doilies, a table cloth, knickknacks wrapped in newspaper. Nothing of hers, thank goodness.

"Hey, Mandy, bring down a box!"

Nick's voice startled her. Quickly she stuffed things back into place. She heard a soft thump— something had fallen out—a book of some sort. She would get it later. Mandy tossed on the lid and scurried down the stairs with the box. She dumped it in her cousin's arms. "Here you go," she said.

Back in the attic, she lifted the lids of the remaining boxes to get a quick look at what was inside. Mostly junk, she decided. Wait, what was that? A piece of yellowed paper caught her attention. She fished it out and unfolded it, being careful not to tear it. A map. The lettering was faded and spidery. There didn't seem to be any 'X marks the spot'. But still, it could be a treasure map.

"Mandy, hurry up!" Nick's voice boomed up the stairs.

She slid the paper into her back pocket. "Coming!" she yelled. She grabbed a box and thudded down the stairs to where her cousin was waiting.

"Aunt Susan says she needs to be there by 9:00 a.m. and to speed it up."

"Okay, okay." Mandy wiped her dusty hands on her jeans and scampered up the stairs. Later she would take a closer look at the map. . . when Nick wasn't around.

Soon, all the boxes were loaded into the minivan. The children hopped in and Mrs. Morrison drove to the town square. The nearest parking space was a block away from Union Hall.

"Bucket brigade!" Mrs. Morrison announced.

Before the first box had made it, hand to hand, to the door of Union Hall, other people had stepped in to help. Strong hands lifted a box from Mandy's arms.

"Here, let me take that, Miss Mandy."

Mandy glanced up into the smiling face of Officer Bailey. He was a good friend of her father's and often stopped by for a game of chess on his evening off. Mandy had a sudden thought. If anyone would know about recent crimes, he would. "Thanks," she said. Trying to sound casual, she asked, "Been any bank robberies today?"

He chuckled. "Not that I've heard. But the day is still young. The banks don't open until nine."

"Oh . . . true." For that matter, she thought, it wouldn't have to be a bank. "How about a convenience store? Or a gas station?"

"If I hear anything, I'll let you know," the policeman said. "Do you want to join the force?" He ruffled her hair and strolled off toward the station.

"Right," she muttered. "May the Force be with you."

All morning, Mandy and Nick were in demand, unpacking boxes, pricing items, helping customers carry their purchases to their cars. It seemed that everyone in town had turned out for the sale. Mandy's despair was growing by the minute. She had to get to the lighthouse. The squatters could commit their crime and return anytime. Her growling stomach gave her an idea.

"Mom, aren't you hungry? How about if I run to Sylvester's and buy subs for the three of us?"

"Good idea," her mother agreed. She opened her purse and dug out some bills. "No dawdling," she warned, handing her daughter the money.

Mandy dodged out the door and flew down the sidewalk to the public wharf. It felt good to be free. The line at Sylvester's was long. A good excuse to dash out to the lighthouse first. When she got back, the line was bound to be shorter. Hands in her pockets, she ambled toward the path. As soon as the waterfront was out of sight, she started jogging.

At the lighthouse, she scrabbled under the porch, propped up the window, and slid through the opening. Dim light filtered through the cellar windows, revealing the gray everyday objects that had seemed so sinister the night before.

Mandy bumped through the clutter. At the foot of the stairs she stopped to listen. There was still the sound of dripping. . . but no sound from above. She tiptoed up the stairs and opened the creaking door. This led into the kitchen of the keeper's house. Right there on the countertop was a big box the squatters had carried in. She peeked inside. Crackers, cans of soup, a box of macaroni, a jug of water, other food. And on top, looking out-of-place, a red plastic firetruck.

Chapter 7: An Ancient Message

Back at Union Hall, Mandy delivered the subs to her mother.

"Things have slowed down a bit," Mrs. Morrison said. "Why don't you and Nick take your sandwiches out to the square to eat?"

"Thanks, Mom," Mandy replied, glad to have a chance to go back outside. It was a perfect June day with a sky of robin's egg blue and a few puffs of white cloud sailing above. A gentle breeze blew a stray wisp of Mandy's hair across her face. How she wished she could be out on the water! In her mind, Little Crumple floated like a distant tantalizing mirage. The treasure—if there *was* a treasure—was waiting. She had to get there soon.

A powerful sneeze from her cousin brought her back to earth. "Pollen," he explained, glancing at the trees whispering overhead. He had already eaten half of his ham and cheese.

Mandy set her sub on the bench between them. "Nick, I went back to the lighthouse. Looks like you were right. Those people are planning to stay for awhile—they brought groceries.

And something else." She told him about the toy firetruck.

"Weird," he commented, and took another bite. He chewed for awhile, thinking about the toy, and then his face cleared. "They must have a kid."

This did not seem likely to Mandy. "So where was he then?" she demanded.

"I don't know," Nick mumbled around his sandwich. "Maybe they got a babysitter."

Mandy rolled her eyes. "Right," she said.

"The Flash for the Fourth was a rip-roaring success," Mrs. Morrison announced that evening at dinner. "We raised enough money to have the best fireworks display Dyer Cove has ever seen!"

"Hooray!" Mandy cheered. Her thoughts drifted to other Fourth of Julys. Her grandfather had always marched in the parade with the other war veterans, tall and proud in his uniform. Eating her mother's strawberry shortcake at the afternoon picnic and raising his spoon for emphasis, he would say, "Jumpin' Jehosophat, this is a little bit of heaven." Her mother would blush and smile at the compliment every time. To top off the wonderful day, there were the fireworks. When Mandy was little, Papa Gene would hold his big hands over her ears to muffle the booms that shook her stomach. Together, they watched the sparkling strings of jewels over the cove, colors made doubly bright by the reflections in the water. They would join in the oohs and aahs and applause of the audience. Mandy's heart ached at the thought of watching the fireworks without him.

"What do you think, Nick?" her father was saying. "Would you like to see the Seadogs play?"

Mandy had drifted right out of the dinner conversation on her sea of memories. Now she returned with a jolt.

"Sure, Uncle Mark," Nick replied. "When is the game?"

Mr. Morrison set down his fork. "Tomorrow afternoon. How about it, Mandy? We'll treat Nick to a *real* hotdog, the kind you can only find in Maine."

Mandy's thoughts warred in her brain. She *loved* baseball. And she could almost taste the red, snappy hotdog smothered in mustard. Seeing the Seadogs play in Portland was pretty special, but if she didn't go, she could do things alone, *without Nick*. She could row out to the island. Her eyes widened. *The map! It was still in her pocket.* "Uh, I think I'll stay home with Mom," she said.

Her father looked surprised. "Are you sure?"

She nodded, not meeting his eyes.

"Well, okay then. It will be the boys' day out."

Once the dishes were done, Mandy dashed upstairs to her room, clicking the lock shut. At last! She unfolded the map and spread it on her bed, being careful not to tear the brittle yellowed paper. The ink was faded and hard to decipher in places, but it seemed to resemble the horseshoe outline of Little Crumple. She searched until her eyes hurt for an 'X marks the spot', but there was nothing. Nothing except some strange markings in the corner of the map. Strange, and yet, somehow familiar. Where had she seen them before? She traced them over and over with her fingertip. Like Egyptian hieroglyphs, she thought. A light flicked on in her mind.

From under the bed, Mandy pulled out the dolphin chest and fished out the key her grandfather had given her. She laid the key with its engraved marks next to the map. The writing on both seemed much alike. What could it mean? Papa Gene had said, 'I feel it in my bones that the answer to the mystery is there.' Little Crumple. Tomorrow she would go to the island. She would find the answer.

Chapter 8: The Island Beckons

"Great day for a ball game," Mr. Morrison commented the next morning at breakfast. "Are you sure you don't want to go, Mandy?" He waggled his eyebrows at her.

She tried not to laugh. "Yes, Dad, I'm sure."

"So how are you planning to spend this gorgeous day?" her mother asked.

"Well, uh, out on the water," Mandy murmured. "I'll probably go fishing."

"Be sure to check with Uncle Gabe," her father reminded her. "So that he'll know you're out there."

"And wear your life vest," her mother added.

Before Mandy could escape, her cousin stopped her in the hall.

"I thought this might be yours," Nick said, holding out a piece of paper. "I found it on the stairs."

She stared at it with horror. It was the copy she had made of the strange marks. She didn't want to risk getting the map wet by taking it in the boat. Mandy snatched it out of his hand.

"So what are you doing with runes?" he said.

"Runes?" she asked, puzzled.

"Yeah, ancient Norse writing. You know, the Vikings?"

"How do you know about that stuff?" Mandy fired back, trying to cover her confusion.

"I did a report for school—Erik the Red, and all that. Did you know the Vikings traveled to this part of the world long before Columbus accidentally discovered America?"

"Uh, no, I didn't know that," Mandy mumbled.

"In fact," Nick continued, "they supposedly landed along the coast of Maine—maybe even at Dyer Cove. . . . So where did you get the runes?"

Mandy did *not* want to tell Nick about the map. "Well, I found it in some old papers. Can you tell what it says?"

Her cousin shook his head. "No, but I bet you could get a book at the library that has the runic alphabet or do a search online. Then you could decode it."

Mandy's eyes widened. "Gee, thanks for the tip. . . And, uh, have a good time at the game." She stuffed the paper in her pocket and hurried out the door. Mandy threw on her small backpack and jogged toward the waterfront. Wow, if she could figure out what the runes said, she would probably know where to search for the treasure. Too bad the library was closed. Hmmmm. What did she know about Vikings? They were fierce fighters, wore those hats with the horns on them, sailed on ships with a dragon head prow and striped sails. They must have had lots of loot, including gold, from raiding all those villages.

Her mind was whirring and her feet picked up the pace. By the time Mandy reached Main Street, she was practically flying down the side-walk. One minute there was nothing in front of her, the next she hit what felt like a brick wall.

Oomph! The air rushed out of her. She gasped like a landed fish.

"Whoa there, Miss Mandy," said Officer Bailey, straightening his cap with one hand and steadying her with the other. "Where's the fire?"

"Oh," she said, when she could breathe again. "I'm sorry. I didn't see you."

"No damage done," he reassured her. "Are you okay?"

"I'm fine. Just rattled my teeth a little."

"By the way," he confided. "Still quiet in the crime world. A shoplifter got nabbed in Bangor and a kidnapping was reported in Boston. Nothing much happening here." He winked at her. "I'll keep you posted."

In all the excitement over the map, Mandy had forgotten about the mysterious couple at the lighthouse. "Uh, thanks, Officer Bailey. Nice running into you," she joked, flashing him a smile.

At a slower pace, she rounded the corner and headed toward the waterfront. Uncle Gabe's fish shack perched above the pier, its weathered shingles silvery in the sunlight. A pyramid of wire traps was stacked by the door, waiting to be repaired. Out on the water, her uncle's white and red lobster boat bobbed at its mooring. Even from here, she could read the name on the bow— *Sea Hag*—painted in bold, black letters. Her own small boat, *Raven,* was tied to the wharf, alongside Uncle Gabe's dory.

Mandy could hear his cheerful whistling. She stuck her head inside the doorway of the fish shack. "Hi, Uncle Gabe," she called. "I'm taking out the boat."

"Hey, Mary Dee," he retorted, using his pet name for her. "Where you headed?"

She grabbed a fishing pole and her life vest from hooks on the wall. "Out to Little Crumple. Going to explore a bit."

"You be careful out there," her uncle warned. "Keep an eye on the tide. You don't want to get stranded."

"Aye, aye, Sir," she promised, giving him a jaunty salute.

Down on the wharf, she buckled on her life jacket and tossed her backpack into the skiff. Soon, she was dodging boats at their moorings, rowing out of the cove. She passed the point where the lighthouse stood, tall and white, its light blinking even though it was daytime. Mandy paused for a moment and shipped the oars so she could peer through binoculars. The lighthouse looked deserted. The squatters didn't seem to be in a hurry to return.

She gripped the oars again and settled down to a steady rhythm. Little Crumple, her destination, beckoned in the distance. What would she find there? Papa Gene hadn't found the treasure. Would she?

Chapter 9: A Discovery

As Mandy neared Little Crumple, she pulled the binoculars out again to scan the island. It was quite small—about the size of two football fields—and in the shape of a horseshoe. She headed for the inside curve, a small sandy beach, which was the only safe place to land. Mandy remembered that from the one time she had been there on a school outing.

She rowed up to the shore, laid the oars in the boat, and jumped into the shallows. Bone-chilling cold sloshed around her ankles. "Yahoo!" she yelled. "Little Crumple—at last!" How she had looked forward to this moment. Mandy tied the long bow line to a stout stump of driftwood lodged in the sand at the high water mark. The tide would turn in about an hour.

"That ought to do it," she said, removing her life vest and wedging it under the driftwood. She lifted out her backpack and tugged it on. "About three hours before *Raven* will be grounded. Plenty of time to explore."

From the top of a tall spruce, a crow cawed at her. At the same moment a cloud drifted in front of the sun, darkening the land. The bird cried another harsh call, spread its large black wings and flapped over her head, as if warning her away. A shiver ran its icy fingers down Mandy's back. For a moment, she had the urge to jump back in the boat and row away. But, no, it had taken her so long to get here. She thought of Papa Gene coming here to search for clues of the shipwreck many years ago. Knowing he had stood in this exact spot gave her courage to go on.

"It's just an old crow," she scolded herself. "There's nothing to be afraid of."

She pushed her way through the low bushes. A faint trail wound through the blueberry and juniper plants and into the forested part of the island. A thick carpet of spruce needles on the path muffled Mandy's footsteps. It was quiet here... so quiet. She remembered the ruins of an old house where some long ago islander had lived. That seemed like a good place to start.

Her grandfather had told her about the Little Crumple hermit. The old man had lived here with only his sheep for company. And died here—alone. Mandy shivered again. Not another ghost, she hoped.

When Mandy reached the spot, she stopped and surveyed her surroundings. The branches of ancient trees met overhead in a dense canopy that blocked much of the light. Gradually, her eyes adjusted to the dimness. What was left of the wooden structure had fallen into the cellar hole in a jumble of rotting timbers. Alders and vines twined around them.

Stones had tumbled out of one side of the wall, forming a rough stairway. Testing each rock to be sure it didn't roll, Mandy worked her way down. The bottom was a tangle of thick growth. Her nose twitched at the sour smell of damp earth and decay. *Like a grave.* Shaking off the morbid thought, she broke off a branch and used it to hack at the vines.

"I am Ponce de Leon, blazing a trail through the wild jungle!" she shouted, wielding her make-shift machete. "Take that! And that!" After a few minutes of energetic whacking, there was little to show for her efforts. The vegetation closed around her like a suffocating blanket. Drops of sweat dribbled between her shoulder blades. "No one could find anything here without a chainsaw and a backhoe," she muttered.

She became aware of an unnatural silence. Her nerves began to tingle. She was not alone. Someone was watching her. Slowly, her eyes searched the trees around the rim of the cellar hole. There by the big pine—was that a figure looking down at her?

"Who's there?" she called out.

In the shadows above, something moved. Mandy swallowed a lump in her throat.

"Hello?"

She clambered back onto the stone stairway to get a better look. A rock under her foot wobbled and she grasped at the wall to steady herself. But the cellar wall itself was unstable. The stone she held onto tumbled out, taking her with it. Down she crashed. Pebbles and dirt cascaded around her. She lay spread-eagle on the ground, the rock pinning her ankle. When she tried to move it, lightning bolts of pain flashed up her leg.

"Help!" she cried. "Whoever's up there, please help me. I'm stuck." A thought struck her. Maybe it *was* a ghost. Do ghosts ever *help* people, she wondered?

Gritting her teeth, Mandy tried again to move her trapped foot. Again pain darted up her leg. She moaned in frustration. Her eyes focused on movement about three feet away. *Was the ground moving?*

"Oh, jumpin' Jehosophat," she whispered, squeezing her eyes shut. A terrible fascination pried one eyelid open. Her worst nightmare unreeled in front of her like an old horror movie. Black shapes wriggled under the vines, twisting and turning around each other—a living, moving sculpture of evil. "Snakes," she said out loud. "I *hate* snakes."

A cold sweat drenched her body. Her heart raced, hammering in her chest. Now she knew how Indiana Jones felt in the pit of snakes. How did he get out of there anyway? She couldn't remember.

"Papa Gene, help," she pleaded. "What do I do?"

One of the snakes freed itself from the writhing mass and crawled toward her. Mandy's eyes widened. "No," she pleaded, "Please, no." Her left arm was stretched out in front of her, but she couldn't pull it back. The long black form slithered over her frozen fingers. The feel of the reptile's dry, heavy body made her skin crawl. Mandy screamed. With strength born of fear, she yanked herself out from under the rock and stumbled to her feet. She kicked the snake away from her. It landed back in the churning heap. Her ankle throbbed. She couldn't put her full weight on it.

It didn't matter. *Nothing* would keep her in this place. She snatched her stick off the ground and propping herself up, hobbled up the rock slide.

Another stone wobbled. Her stomach flip-flopped at the thought of falling back into that evil pit. Mandy grabbed at the broken edge of the cellar wall to catch her balance. Something was sticking out on top of a rock—a small bundle wrapped in a dark, greasy cloth.

"How strange."

For a moment she forgot the snakes. Steadying herself, she picked up the packet and shook off the loose dirt. Someone must have hidden it in the cellar wall a long time ago. Clutching it close, she continued to climb. Near the top, she teetered on a rock and thrust out both hands to keep from tumbling. The bundle sailed through the air and landed somewhere under the big green leaves down in the pit.

"No *way* am I going back down there for that thing," she said. "At least not now." She grabbed a root sticking out of the ground and pulled herself out of the cellar hole.

Mandy hobbled along the path to the beach, wincing at each step. She kept looking over her shoulder, expecting some unearthly form to be right behind her. She couldn't wait to get out of this place. Mandy cleared the bushes and stumbled into the sand. She stopped short. Something was missing. Something *important* was missing. Her bright orange life vest was still lodged under the stump. *The boat was gone.*

Chapter 10: Stranded!

Mandy limped along the small beach, hoping. Hoping she was imagining this. How could the boat be gone? She dug through her backpack for the binoculars. Focusing first on the distant sparkling waves and then sweeping closer, she spotted movement. There! About a hundred yards away the boat bobbed, its bow headed toward the mainland like a horse bolting for the stable without its rider.

"Shoot!" exclaimed Mandy. She knew she had two choices—sit still and wait to be rescued, which, of course, meant she would never be allowed out on the water alone again *or* swim for it. Could she swim with a sprained ankle?

"One way to find out," she mumbled. Mandy dumped the backpack in the sand and strapped on her life vest. Clenching her teeth, she stepped into the icy water. "Okay, you can do this," she told herself. She struck out with strong overhand strokes. Her ankle hurt at first, but not for long. The sea water was so cold it soon numbed her ankle, not to mention the rest of her.

Bit by bit, Mandy gained on the skiff. "You can do it," she told herself. She wasn't the best swimmer in the world. And she was getting tired. She thought of how her mother would worry if someone found the empty boat. She rested for a moment, her life vest keeping her afloat. She dug deeper for the strength to keep going. "Almost there."

Something brushed against her bare leg. Was it an eel? A *shark*? She fought down the panic that started bubbling in her stomach and forced herself to take steady strokes. "One. . .two. . .three. . ." she counted to keep the fear under control.

At last, her fingertips brushed against the bowline, which was floating out behind the boat. She grasped the rope and pulled herself along until she could touch the skiff itself. Now to get in. Mandy reached up to the edge of the stern.

"Ready, set . . . go!" she cried, and thrust herself out of the water. Panting and shivering, she sprawled in the boat. "Yes," she whispered. "Did it."

With aching arms, Mandy rowed back to the island to retrieve her backpack. From the position of the sun, she could tell it was about three o'clock. Hunger pains clawed at her stomach like a starving animal. Once again she tied *Raven* to the stump.

"Food," she moaned. "I can't row any further without food."

She shrugged her sweatshirt on over goose-bumped arms and then found lunch in the bottom of her backpack. She wolfed down the squished peanut butter and jelly sandwich and gulped half a bottle of water. A little bit at a time, her chilled body thawed out and her limbs stopped shaking. "That's better," she said. Mandy bit into a granola bar and began thinking about the mysterious bundle back there in the cellar hole. Maybe it was nothing. But it had looked old and it had been stashed in the cellar wall. *Someone* must have thought it was important. Did it belong to the old hermit? Or had someone else hidden it there? Maybe it was the treasure she had been hoping to find for so long. Or maybe it had something to do with the key her grandfather had given her. Should she go back? A vision of the churning mass of black snakes filled her mind. Mandy shuddered. She just *couldn't* go back into that pit of writhing reptiles. Not to mention the ghostly presence. There had to be another way.

Mandy glanced up at the skiff. The tide was still going out and the boat was about to be stranded on the sand. Time to shove off. Grunting, she pushed the boat until it was afloat again, hopped in and headed for home.

The beam of the lighthouse winked at her as she rowed past the point. As she had on the way out, Mandy stopped for a moment and focused the binoculars on the keeper's house. Nothing stirring, except a gull perched on the rooftop. Wait . . . what was that? Mandy moved the glasses back to the kitchen window. A pale form seemed to be looking out. One of the squatters maybe? . . . Or the ghost of old Captain Kimball? Mandy shivered. She would have to go back to the lighthouse soon to investigate.

By the time she reached the wharf, her hair and clothes were dry. No explanation needed for her misadventure. Her uncle wasn't in the fish house so Mandy stowed the oars and life jacket and closed the door. Uncle Gabe would know she had returned when he saw *Raven* at its mooring.

At home, she breezed through the front door. "Mom, I'm home!" she called. Mandy was hoping she could make it to her room without being seen, but no such luck.

"Hold it right there, young lady," her mother's voice commanded.

Mandy turned to look at her mother who stood, hands on hips, in the kitchen doorway.

"Where have you been all this time? I was getting worried about you." Mrs. Morrison surveyed her daughter's wild curling hair, scraped knees and salt-encrusted skin.

"Uh, I rowed out to Little Crumple. . . It was such a beautiful day. Dad said I could when I was ten," she babbled.

"What if something had happened to you?" her mother demanded.

If you only knew, Mandy thought. But what she said was, "I can take care of myself."

"You are *not* to go out there alone again. Do you understand?"

"But, Mom."

"*Mandy?*"

"Yes, ma'am," she murmured, looking at the floor.

Shoot, shoot, and double shoot! Mandy thought, as she trudged up the stairs to her room. Now how would she find the treasure?

Chapter 11: The Meaning of the Map

"You missed a great game, Mandy," her father said as he spooned a dollop of mashed potato on his plate. "The Seadogs beat the Navigators 6-5." He drizzled gravy over the potato and roast beef. "You should have seen Sandberg's homerun. It was a sight to see, wasn't it, Nick?"

Nick nodded. "It was outta there! And you should have seen the fans. There was this group dressed up like pirates. They went wild. I thought they were going to flatten the mascot—Snugger, is it? They were whooping and hollering and jumping all over the place."

"And what did *you* do on this fine day?" Mr. Morrison continued.

"Well, I spent the day out on the water. It was beautiful out there." Mandy cast an anxious glance at her mother, but Mrs. Morrison was occupied with slipping a strawberry pie out of the oven.

"Did you catch anything?" Nick asked.

Mandy thought of the mysterious bundle that had fallen into the snake pit. "I almost had a big one, but it got away."

"Isn't that always the way?"

"So what's happening in the news?" Mandy asked her father, changing the subject. He had just snapped off the television set before dinner.

Mr. Morrison chewed while he considered. "Let's see. A big grass fire in Trenton. A rescue on Mt. Katahdin. A kidnapping in Boston."

"No robberies?"

Her father raised an eyebrow. "Now that you mention it, there was a convenience store robbery in Bangor. "Why do you ask?"

Mandy pushed a green bean around with her fork, trying to hide her excitement. *Were the lighthouse squatters the thieves?* "Just wondering."

After dinner, Mandy and Nick were left alone to do the dishes. "Hey, Mandy, I've got something to show you," Nick said. "Meet me on the porch. Oh, and bring your map."

She stared at him. "Map? What map?" How did he find out?

"The one with the runes on it. Aunt Susan asked me to drop off some laundry and I saw the map on your bed."

"You were in my room?" she asked, trying not to panic.

"Hey, just following orders. So bring the map."

"Why?" she demanded with suspicion in her voice.

"You'll see," Nick replied. He headed down the hall to her father's study.

Great, Mandy thought. Now what do I do? She did *not* want to show her cousin the map. But if he could shed some light on it, she sure wanted to know. She climbed the stairs, still limping from her fall in the cellar hole, and retrieved the map. How could she have been so careless as to leave it on her bed?

On the porch, Nick held a thick book in his hands—her father's dictionary. "Look at this," he said, opening the volume where a slip of paper marked a page. "I thought I would try looking up 'runes'. Bingo."

Mandy's heart lurched as she studied the strange letters on the page. They were much like the writing on the map. . . and on the key her grandfather had given her. Beneath each symbol was the English letter it represented.

Mandy unfolded the map with trembling fingers. Together she and Nick studied the marks in the corner of the map, comparing them with the code in the book.

"Look!" That's an H," her cousin exclaimed. He jotted it down on a notepad.

"Next one's an E," said Mandy, pointing to an M-shaped rune.

The faded writing on the map was hard to make out in places, but for most of the letters they found a match.

"H-E-something-R-T, O-F something-O-L-D," muttered Nick.

"Heart!" yelled Mandy. It has to be HEART! Heart of __OLD. She started through the alphabet. "Bold, cold, fold, . . .gold."

"That's it, Mandy! See, the G has two symbols combined. HEART OF *GOLD*!" He stared at her, amazement dawning on his face. "It's a treasure map!" His voice took on an accusing note. "But you knew that, didn't you?"

"Well, I thought it might be, but I wasn't sure. . . until now." Mandy began to slide the map out from under his hand.

"Wait," Nick demanded. "Do you know where this place is? It looks like an island."

Mandy's mind was reeling. The secret was out. Nick was the last person she wanted as a treasure-hunting partner, but she did need *someone* to go with her back to the island. Reaching a decision, she said, "Let me ask *you* a question. How do you feel about snakes?"

"Snakes? They're okay. In fact, I *like* snakes. . . except the poisonous ones. My best friend at home has a pet python. It's great watching it eat."

Mandy rolled her eyes. It figured the guy would actually *like* snakes.

He was weird, no question about it. But he was just what she needed at the moment. "We don't have poisonous snakes in Maine," she informed him. "And the island on the map is Little Crumple."

Chapter 12: The Key Decoded

Mandy tiptoed to the study to get the dictionary her cousin had replaced on the shelf. The symbols on the key needed to be deciphered, too. She didn't have to tell Nick *everything*. As she reached for the book, she heard voices in the hallway.

"Tonight's the night. I feel a victory coming on," her father was saying.

The door swung open. Mr. Morrison led Officer Bailey to the small table where the chess pieces stood in orderly rows.

"Oh, Dad," Mandy spoke up. "I'm just getting the dictionary. Hi, Officer Bailey."

"Hello there, Miss Mandy. Just the person I wanted to see. Did you hear about last night's robbery in Bangor?"

Mandy set the heavy volume on her father's desk. "Yes, Dad told me. How much did they get?"

"Not much. About $300. There's a description going out to the media—a tall, thin young man, about 18 or 19. Thought you'd want to know the details." He winked at her.

"Why the sudden interest in robberies, Mandy?" her father asked. "Do you know something we don't?"

Mandy considered telling them about the couple at the lighthouse. But the description of the robber didn't seem to fit either Mike or Suze. She sure didn't want to get innocent people in trouble. If they *were* innocent. She would have to do further investigating at the lighthouse. Soon. "Uh, no, I don't know anything," she replied. "I hope the police catch him."

"Oh, they will," assured Officer Bailey. "It's just a matter of time."

Mandy toted the dictionary up to her room and flipped the pages to the runic alphabet. She fetched the key from the dolphin box. The marks on the key were tiny, but with a magnifying glass she was able to decipher the word *FREYA*. What on earth was that? She turned the pages back to **F** and there it was—*Freya: Norse goddess of love and beauty.* Mandy stroked the key with her forefinger. Where did it come from? The Vikings had lived a long time ago. Why would it have been hanging in the lighthouse? The answers might never be found. There did seem to be a connection, though, between the key and map. It was too much of a coincidence that they both were decorated with runes.

Mandy rummaged in her desk drawer for a piece of string and found instead an old shoelace with dolphins on it. That seemed fitting. She threaded it through the loop on the top of the key and tied it around her neck. "There," she muttered to herself. "The key is sticking with me."

That night as she lay in bed, Mandy held the key in her hand. She wondered about the person who had owned it. Was her name Freya? Was she beautiful with long golden hair and a sunny smile? How did the key get from Freya to old Captain Kimball's pocket? Mandy drifted off to sleep, dreaming of Viking ships and treasure and snakes.

In the morning, Mandy found Nick in the kitchen pouring milk on his cornflakes. "Hey, Nick," she said in a casual voice. "Would you like to go out in the boat today?'

"Well, I—" he started.

"To the island . . . . . . with the map," she added.

He stared at her, his eyes growing wide. "To look for treasure?"

Mandy nodded her head. "We'll leave in about a half hour. I just need to find something first."

An idea had blinked into her brain while she slept. Now she dashed up the stairs to the attic. Somewhere up here she remembered seeing a pair of waders—probably the pair Papa Gene used to go clam-digging on the mudflats. As she searched behind a stack of boxes, her foot hit against something on the floor. Mandy reached into the shadows and felt around until her fingers found a rectangular object. She picked it up and held it so that light from the window, dancing with dust motes, shone on it. A book. An *old* book with a worn, brown leather cover. That must be what fell out of the box the day she was carrying stuff for the rummage sale. It looked like a diary—maybe her grandfather's or grandmother's. That would be interesting reading. She would look at it later.

Mandy could see the tall, rubber boots slumped behind a chest. She grabbed them and headed downstairs, tucking the book under her arm. She stopped at her bedroom door and tossed the book on her bed. The waders were too big for her, of course, but if she rolled the tops over and pulled the boots on over her shoes, she could probably keep them on.

"Look out snakes," she murmured. "Here I come."

Chapter 13: Back to the Island

"You two be careful out there!" Uncle Gabe warned as he handed them both a life vest. "Weather's brewin'."

"But the sun's shining and the water's like glass," Mandy protested.

"Mary Dee, you've lived in Maine long enough to know how fast the weather can change. He rumpled her hair. "See that haze there on the horizon?" he said to Nick. "That can move in mighty quick. Just get the little lady back here in a couple of hours."

Nick snickered and Mandy glared at him.

"Here," she said, thrusting the oars into his hands. "Let's go. You do know how to row, don't you?"

"Sure, I do." My family goes camping at the lake back home... I've rowed a few times."

As they headed toward Little Crumple, Mandy had to admit that her cousin could row. At first he was clumsy, splashing her with the oars, but then he settled down into a regular rhythm.

As they passed the point, Nick glanced at the lighthouse. "I wonder if the squatters are back. They couldn't have planned to be gone long since they brought groceries."

Mandy scanned the windows of the keeper's house, one by one, with the binoculars. No movement there. "We need to check it out. . . tonight."

"*We?*" Nick said. "Why do you keep dragging *me* into this? And why do we always have to go there at *night?*" He slapped an oar against the water and a glistening cascade showered Mandy.

"Nick!" she squealed through gritted teeth. She used the side of her hand to squeegee water off her face. "Are you afraid the *ghosts* will get you?"

He scowled at her. "No. . . I suppose you need someone to protect you."

Mandy rolled her eyes. "Whatever," she mumbled. At least it sounded as if he would come. She wouldn't admit it to him, of course, but having him along would make her ten times braver. If there was a ghost out there, it would run the other way when Nick came bumbling through.

They didn't speak to each other for the next fifteen minutes. Nick rowed steadily toward the island. As they neared the beach, Mandy hopped out and grabbed the bowline. The boat scraped bottom. Nick jumped out and together they dragged the skiff up onto the sand.

"A little further," Mandy urged.

Her cousin grunted and gave the boat one last heave. Mandy wound the rope around and around the stump and tied knot after knot.

Nick watched, hands on hips. "Are you afraid the boat's going to float away or something? We'll need an ax to get it loose."

She pulled the last knot extra tight. "This boat's not going *anywhere*. . . this time," she added to herself.

They shucked their life vests and Mandy reached into the boat for the waders.

"What are *those* for?" Nick asked with amusement. "Are you going to dig for treasure or dig for clams?"

"Never mind," Mandy retorted. She stalked off down the path.

At the edge of the old cellar hole, she stopped and peered down into the jungle of growth. "Shoot," she murmured. The mysterious packet was not in plain sight, as she had hoped it would be. She could send Nick the Fearless down to search for it, but she didn't trust him. He might open it right there in the snake pit. She had a feeling in her bones, as her grandfather used to say, that it was the treasure. She wanted to be the one to open it after all her dreams of finding it.

Mandy pulled the tall rubber boots on over her water shoes and rolled the tops down.

Nick's eyebrows rose as he tried to figure out what she was doing. Then it dawned on him. He burst out laughing. "Snakes! You're going to wade through the snakes, aren't you?" The harder he laughed, the redder Mandy's face got.

"Shut up!" she ordered. "You go first."

"Yes, your majesty," Nick replied, sweeping off an imaginary hat and mocking her with a bow.

As he turned his back on her, Mandy was tempted to kick him in the behind. But she resisted. It was hard enough keeping her footing in the awkward waders. Stone by stone, she shuffled downward. Nick was already at the bottom. In her hurry to catch up to him, she forgot about the wobbly rock.

"Whoa!" she yelled, as the stone rolled under her foot. Mandy pitched headfirst, flying through the air and crashing into Nick. They fell in a tangled heap.

"Get off me, Mandy!" her cousin shouted. "What's the matter with you?" He struggled out from under her.

Mandy lay where she was, her eyes intent on what was in front of her. Underneath a big leaf about three yards away rested the mysterious packet. Curled around it like a hangman's noose was the biggest, blackest snake Mandy had ever seen.

Chapter 14: The Treasure

The snake's head turned to stare at Mandy. Its beady black eyes held her gaze, hypnotizing her. Its tongue flicked, as if warning her to stay away.

Nick's voice broke the spell. "Are you okay?" He stopped brushing the dirt off his jeans and gaped at her motionless form. "Mandy?"

"Look, there it is," she whispered.

Her cousin glanced in the direction she was pointing. "There *what* is?" He spied the reptile-wrapped package. "Wow, what a beaut. I don't suppose we can take him home?" Nick crouched to get a better look. The snake raised its head and stared at him. still flicking its tongue.

"Not the snake, Nick. . . the package," Mandy answered. "The treasure."

His eyes blinked in disbelief. *"That's* the treasure?"

"I think so, yes. It fell out of the wall the last time I was here."

Nick whistled. "Cool. Well, let's get it!"

"Careful," Mandy warned. "Snakes do bite, poisonous or not. He's not going to let go without a fight." She raised herself to a sitting position.

Her cousin broke a branch from a young alder and stripped off the leaves. He inched toward the snake. Just as he was about to prod it with the stick, a scream shattered the silence. Nick whirled, dropping the stick.

"Aaaaaaaaah! *There's something in my boot!*" Mandy screeched. She jumped up. Something was wriggling against her bare leg inside the wader. She hopped from one foot to the other, her eyes wide with terror. "Help!"

"Sit down," Nick ordered.

Mandy continued to hop. Nick pushed her over. He got hold of a boot and yanked it off.

"The other one, Nick!" she said, still squirming.

He reached for the other wader and pulled it off more slowly. He turned the boot upside down. A small snake dropped out and slithered off. "He was just looking for his mommy," Nick joked.

Mandy's face was dark as a thundercloud. "Fun-*nee*," she retorted. "I am *not* his mother. Nor will I ever be *any* snake's mother. I *hate* snakes! I have had it with snakes." She scrambled to her feet, still shaking. "Where's that stick?" She snatched

Nick's branch from the ground, marched over to the packet and poked at the snake guarding it. "Get lost!" she yelled. "Go find your own treasure!" The reptile hissed and flicked, but Mandy kept prodding it until it uncoiled and slid away. She hugged the packet to her in triumph. "Let's get out of here."

Back at the beach, they plopped down in the warm sand.

"Open it," Nick urged. "I want to see the treasure."

What Mandy really wanted to do was take the packet home and open it in the privacy of her room—alone. But, after all they had been through, Nick did deserve to see it.

She dug her jackknife out of the backpack and cut the cord holding the package together. With eager fingers she unfolded the oilskin wrapping, revealing a small wooden chest the size of her mother's recipe box. Her fingers trembled. What could be inside? Gold coins? Jewels? Would they be rich? She tried to lift the lid. "It's locked."

"Pry it open with your knife," Nick suggested.

Mandy held the box up to her face. Her fingertips had felt indentations in the wood. She studied it closely. Words. Words written in runes.

"No need to force it," she murmured. "I think I've got the key."

"You do?" Nick asked in surprise. "Where?"

"Here." Mandy pulled the shoestring out of her t-shirt with the key from her dolphin box dangling on it. "I got it from my Papa Gene." She fit the key into the lock and turned it. Holding her breath, she lifted the lid.

Inside there was no gold. No jewels. Just a tarnished silver locket and a slip of paper.

"That's *it?*" Nick exclaimed, his voice thick with disappointment. "*That's* the treasure?"

Her cousin's words echoed in Mandy's head. After all the dreaming, the searching, the scheming, this was it? This was the treasure? Her throat felt tight. She wanted to cry, but she wouldn't in front of Nick. Maybe there was more back in the cellar hole? But Mandy knew in her heart that this was it. The key had fit. This was what she was meant to find.

She picked the yellowed paper from the box. A note written in a hurried but elegant hand read: *In great desperation and as a last hope I send my dear daughter Annie toward the light. I commend her into God's care.* What did it mean? It sounded like a desperate message. Mandy set it back in the chest and lifted the necklace. The chain was blackened, but fashioned of delicate links. From it hung a locket, its oval surface etched with a pattern of flowers and leaves. With a thumbnail she opened it. Inside lay a tiny curl of golden hair. "Freya," Mandy whispered.

Nick had found food in Mandy's backpack and was munching on a granola bar. A fat raindrop splashed on his hand. He glanced up at the sky and gulped. "Oh, no. Mandy, look at that."

They had forgotten Uncle Gabe's warning. Now dark clouds boiled overhead, blocking out the sun.

"We'd better shove off," Nick said. He was already picking at the knots in the rope that held the skiff to the stump. "Why did you tie these so tight, Mandy? We'll never get them undone." He looked at the sky again and moaned.

The rain splattered now, making little craters in the sand. Mandy tucked the necklace back in the box. She rewrapped the chest in the oilskin and stowed it in her backpack. "Here," she said, tossing her jackknife to her cousin. "Just cut it."

They donned their life jackets and pushed the boat into the water. Nick took up the oars and began to row. Once they were out of the protected lea of the island, what they saw frightened them both. To the horizon, the sky was alive with roiling clouds. Rain streaked down in long gray ribbons. A jag of lightning lit the sea with electric starkness revealing a wild expanse of racing whitecaps.

Nick's face was pale and anxious. "Looks bad," he said. "Should we go back to the island?"

Just then the wind hit them with the force of a freight train. The waves deepened. The small boat wallowed from crest to crest. Water sloshed over the sides.

"We can't!" Mandy yelled. "Wind's against us. Head for shore!"

Chapter 15: Lost in the Storm

"Whatever you do, don't let the boat turn broadside," Mandy shouted, gripping the gunwale with white-knuckled fingers. A jag of lightning snaked across the sky, followed by a whip crack of thunder.

Water streamed down Nick's face, plastering his hair to his forehead. He tried to keep the bow headed toward Dyer Cove, but the boat kept slewing sideways in the deepening waves. A whitecap broke over the side. "You've got to bail!" he yelled.

Mandy reached for the small plastic bucket that was tied to the thwart. She scooped at the cold water sloshing around her feet. Scoop. Splash. Scoop. Splash. For every pailful she threw out, another splashed in. "It's hopeless!" she wailed, a note of panic in her voice. But she kept on bailing. "Row faster, Nick!"

Her cousin's face contorted with effort. His biceps bulged as he put every ounce of strength into the oars.

A bigger wave slammed into them, pushing the skiff in a different direction. "Which way do we go, Mandy?" he asked, confused.

Mandy stared at the sea through half-closed eyes. The rain felt like needles on her skin. Her gaze rotated 360 degrees, but the sea looked the same in every direction. They were lost. Mandy's stomach fluttered with fear. She squeezed her eyes shut.

Her thoughts swirled. Through the mists of time, her grandfather's voice echoed in her mind. 'You can storm against what life dishes out to you. . . or you can batten down the hatches and ride out the storm—see where the sea takes you.' Mandy opened her eyes. "Just go with the flow, Nick."

Her cousin looked at her like she had lost her mind. "What do you mean?"

"We'll be okay," she answered, "if we can keep the boat afloat." She started bailing again.

"And if we don't get fried by lightning," Nick mumbled. Another bolt streaked overhead. He concentrated on keeping the stern to the waves so that the wind and sea pushed them along.

Punctuating the noise of the storm was another sound. "Do you hear that?" Nick said. . . "Listen!"

Through the shriek of the wind and rush of the water, Mandy heard a low moan, sounding at regular intervals. "The foghorn!" she said. "We're close to the lighthouse."

"But where is it?" Nick asked. It was hard to tell where the sound was coming from.

"Over there!" Mandy said, pointing.

Nick glanced over his shoulder, just in time to catch a flash that was *not* lightning. A long straight beam sliced through the clouds. No light had ever seemed as welcoming. "All *right*!" He dug in with the oars.

Soon the *Raven* grated on the rocky shore. Slipping on the wet stones, the cousins tugged the vessel as far up on the beach as they could and then collapsed.

"I could kiss the ground," Nick said, slumping down on the side of the boat.

Mandy glanced at him and then peered more closely. Was that rain or tears on his face? "I know what you mean," she agreed. "I thought we were goners. You saved us, Nick."

He looked at her, surprised by the admiration in her voice. "Yeah?"

"Yeah," she said.

Mandy took off her life vest and put on her soaking backpack. "Let's take shelter in the lighthouse," she suggested.

"Let's go home," Nick replied. "I don't see how we can get any wetter than we already are." Thunder cracked nearby. "On the other hand. . ."

Mandy was already clambering up the path to the tower, grasping bushes to keep from sliding down. Nick followed. Another crackle sizzled across the sky, followed by a boom.

"That hit something!" Mandy said. "Come on."

As they rounded the tower, Mandy stopped in her tracks. Nick crashed into her.

"What now?" he asked, rubbing his sore shoulder.

"S-s-sh," she warned. "Look!"

In the kitchen window, a dim light flickered. A dark form passed in front of it.

"The squatters—they're back," Mandy whispered.

Chapter 16: The Haunted Lighthouse

Mandy was tempted to peek through the kitchen window. Were the squatters counting money from a robbery? If she stood on Nick's back, she could probably see in. No, too risky.

"This way," she said, creeping past the window toward the front of the keeper's house.

At the edge of the porch, Mandy crouched down and removed the section of lattice. She disappeared into the dark hole. Nick crawled after her. Under the porch it was pitch black. It was also warm and musty. Mandy's hand grazed a dangling cobweb that clung to her wet skin.

"Try not to sneeze," she whispered. "Your sneezes are loud enough to wake the dead."

"What did you have to say *that* for?" Nick's nose started to tickle. He pinched it shut—hard.

"Let's go in the basement," Mandy whispered.

"Why?" he asked in a nasal tone. I'm fine right here."

Mandy felt around for the cellar window. She tried to lift it. "Maybe"—grunt—"we can hear what they're saying. . . It's stuck. Help me, Nick."

Nick let go of his nose and crept toward his cousin's voice. He found the bottom of the window and pushed it up.

"Don't forget the stick," Mandy said, poking him in the side with it.

"Ouch! Be careful." Nick grabbed the stick and used it to prop up the window. "Boy, I wish we had a light."

No sooner were the words out of his mouth than a tiny penlight beam struck him in the eye.

"Where have you been hiding that?" he asked, shielding his face with his hand.

"I forgot it was in my backpack. Always be prepared—that's *my* motto."

"Right," Nick murmured. "Ladies first."

Mandy slipped through the window and landed on the chair below. She climbed down and shone the light so her cousin could see. Nick dropped down beside her.

"Okay, now what?"

"The stairs are over here," Mandy said. She began threading her way through the piles of junk—old wooden barrels and crates, broken furniture, a rickety floor lamp. Everything looked strange and sinister in the dim light. She shivered, thinking about the ghost of old Captain Kimball. Some of these things had probably been touched by his hands when he was alive. Now he was dead. Long dead. But not gone. Still roaming the lighthouse to keep an eye on what went on there.

The house creaked and groaned in the storm. She could still hear the foghorn moaning, a low mournful cry like that of a dying moose.

"Are you sure there's no ghost?"

Nick's voice, close to her ear, jumped her. Mandy clapped a hand over her racing heart. "Of *course* there's a ghost," she said, with an edge to her voice. "Legends always have some truth in them. I'm sure he's around. . . somewhere."

She crept forward. A white shape loomed in front of her. Mandy gasped and thrust the penlight at it like a sword. The tiny beam danced over the surface of a dressmaker's mannequin. She let out her breath in relief and sidestepped the headless form. "Come on."

Mandy started up the cellar stairs. A line of pale light glowed under the door above.

Nick gripped her arm. "What are you—crazy? You can't go up there!"

"It's the only way we can hear what they're saying," she protested.

Heavy footfalls thumped over their heads.

"Someone's coming," Nick said. He pulled Mandy off the stairs. They hurried behind a stack of barrels and crouched down. "Turn off the light, for Pete's sake!"

Just in time, Mandy hit the off button. At the top of the stairs, the door squealed open on rusty hinges. Lantern light filled the basement. The shadow of a man flickered eerily on the wall. He seemed to be holding something—a bundle of some sort. A pitiful whimper came from the bundle.

Mandy broke out in a cold sweat. Could it be the old lightkeeper and his dying child? She squeezed her eyes shut. *There's no such things as ghosts,* she told herself. *No matter what I tell Nick.*

Chapter 17: The Chase

Nick and Mandy tried to make themselves as small as possible behind the barrels.

The stairs creaked under the weight of the dark figure.

"Stop sniveling," a voice growled. "I can't take anymore."

That's no ghost, Mandy thought. She recognized the voice of the male squatter. Who was he talking to?

"Just shut up and go to sleep. . . or else," the man finished in a menacing tone. He clomped back up the stairs and slammed the door.

"Turn on the light, Mandy," Nick whispered. He glanced at her white face and put a finger to his lips.

They tiptoed to the corner, being careful not to make any noise. On a tattered mattress huddled a small boy about five years old. His cheeks were smudged with dirt. Beside him was the red plastic fire truck. He cowered away from them.

Mandy scooched down. "It's okay," she said. "We're friends. Mandy and Nick. Who are you?"

"Jonathan," whimpered the boy. "I want to go home."

"What are you doing here?" asked Nick.

"The bad man took me away from my nanny. I want Daddy." He stuck his dirty thumb in his mouth and stared at them with big brown eyes.

"You know," Mandy said to her cousin, "my father mentioned that there was a kidnapping on the news. In Boston, I think he said."

"Oh, yeah," Nick said. "I read about it in the paper. Some millionaire's son. The father owns a big-time computer program outfit. The kid got snatched in the park. They suspect a guy who just got fired from the company. Found out he had a history—petty theft, armed robbery."

Mandy gulped. "Armed robbery as in *guns?*"

"Afraid so," Nick said. "What are we going to do?"

"We're going to help Jonathan."

"But they'll kill us!" Nick protested.

"Only if they catch us. . . Come on, Jonathan. We're going to get you out of here." Mandy took the boy's hand and led him to the window. She gave him a boost.

Nick was the last one to climb through. His foot knocked the chair off balance and it crashed over. Under the porch, the children froze. Voices rumbled inside the house. They heard the cellar door open and boots thunder down the stairs.

"The kid! He's getting away," the male kidnapper bellowed.

Mandy's heart jumped in her chest. "He'll see the open window. We need to get out of here." She scrambled to the outside, pulling Jonathan along with her.

"Hurry up, hurry up," Nick urged, behind them.

Outside, the rain had stopped, but dark storm clouds still scudded across the sky.

"We can't take the path," Nick warned. "They'll catch us."

"This way," Mandy said, leading them to the faint trail that wound down to the beach.

"Are we taking the boat?" asked Nick. "We'd be sitting ducks for sure."

"No, come on!" Mandy replied.

They slipped and slid down the slope to the rocky shore. Nick and Mandy each grasped one of Jonathan's hands and helped him across the slippery expanse of seaweed.

"Come back here!" a voice yelled behind them.

A bullet zinged on a nearby rock.

"Good grief, he's shooting!" Mandy cried. "Quick. . . over here!" She dodged behind a rock the size of a car. Peering out, she saw two figures clambering down the bank after them.

Then the kidnappers hit the seaweed. They struggled for footing and fell hard. A string of curses rang through the air.

"What is this stuff?" the woman whined. "I can't walk on this."

Oomph. The man fell again. "Come on," he roared. "We'll get those brats on the path."

As the children watched from behind the boulder, the couple struggled back up the bank to the lighthouse. It was the break Mandy and Nick needed.

"Let's *go!*" she shouted.

They continued across the seaweed, practically carrying Jonathan between them.

Mandy gasped for breath. Her thoughts were whirling. These people were dangerous. Could the three of them get to the path in time? Or would the kidnappers be waiting there with a loaded gun?

Chapter 18: Danger in the Darkness

"You're doing great, Jonathan," Mandy said. "Almost there."

She and Nick lifted the little boy up onto the path. No one was there. They stood still, listening. Further out on the point, twigs cracked and voices murmured. The kidnappers were on their way.

"We need to go right to the police station," Mandy decided. "Come on."

"I'm tired," said Jonathan. "I want my daddy."

"We're going to take you to Daddy. You've got to keep going."

"I can't," he complained, plopping to the ground.

The noises of the furious kidnappers were getting closer.

"Do you want a ride?" Nick asked him in desperation. He crouched down so the boy could climb on his back. "Keep your head low."

Mandy was tugging on a dead birch tree. "This," she grunted, "will slow them down a little." She pulled the big branch across the path. As she looked up, she caught a movement of white in the trees. *What was that?* she wondered. No time to find out now.

The children hurried along the path as Mandy guided them with the penlight. Finally, they reached the parking lot by the public wharf. The lot was empty except for a beat-up, black pick-up. It was parked up against the bushes, making it hard to see. Mandy shone the light on the muddy license plate.

"Massachusetts," Nick exclaimed. "It must be the kidnappers' truck. We should flatten the tires or something so they can't get away."

"We don't have time," Mandy said. "They're almost here."

Loud voices emerged from the woods. "We have to get them, Suze," the man was yelling. "That's our meal ticket!"

"Just let them go," she pleaded. "We need to get out of here."

At that moment, the man caught sight of the children scurrying across the parking lot. He raised the gun to fire.

The woman pushed his arm down. "Don't!" she shouted. "You can't shoot kids!"

Mandy felt a surge of fear. This guy was a lunatic. They *had* to get away. She ducked behind the sub shop. Mandy had one big advantage. She knew every inch of the town. "This way," she whispered to Nick.

Down through the leafy tunnel of Pintail Lane, keeping to the deep shadows. Under the bent corner of Mr. Chase's wire fence and past his stack of lobster traps. Should they stop and knock on his door? No time. They would probably get shot in the back. Keep going. Through Miss Mac-Dougall's rose garden and out onto Main Street.

Where are people when you need them? Mandy wondered. There was no one in sight. But the lights of the police station glowed invitingly. She rushed toward the building, towing Jonathan behind her. Nick was on their heels. The three of them tumbled into the station. Mandy slammed the door shut.

Officer Bailey glanced up from his paperwork. "Well, look what the wind blew in," he said. "Where have you kids been? Your folks are worried sick about you."

Nick and Mandy both spoke at the same time.

"At the lighthouse—"

"The kidnappers—"

"Whoa, slow down," the policeman ordered. "One at a time."

"We were out at Little Crumple and got blown off course by the storm," Mandy explained, "and landed at the lighthouse. The kidnappers had Jonathan prisoner in the basement. This is Jonathan." She gently pushed the little boy forward.

"And the kidnapper is out there with a gun!" added Nick.

"A gun?" asked Officer Bailey. "In Dyer Cove, Maine? You've got to be kidding."

"He was shooting at us on the beach!" Mandy said. "You've got to hurry. They'll get away!"

"Shooting, you say?" asked Officer Bailey, springing into action. "That's enough to pull the guy in for questioning." He spoke into the radio, directing a unit to the waterfront. "Approach with caution," he warned the officers. "Suspect is armed."

"All right, you three, take a seat. While we're waiting, let's sort this out. . . Son," he said to Jonathan in a kind voice, "tell me what happened to you."

The little boy glanced first at Mandy and then at Nick. He huddled close to Nick and put his thumb in his mouth.

"He told us a man took him from his nanny in the park," Nick explained. "The guy and a woman were keeping him in the cellar of the lighthouse."

"Do you know his last name?" the policeman asked.

Mandy knelt down in front of the little boy. "Can you tell me your whole name, Jonathan?"

Jonathan took his thumb out of his mouth and stood a little taller. "Jonathan Edward Truman," he said, "Just like my daddy."

"Ahh," said Officer Bailey. "The Boston kidnapping. I'd better notify the authorities there. And you should call your parents, Mandy," he added. "They'll want to know you're okay."

While Mandy was on the phone talking with her father, the station door opened. Two officers led in the kidnappers in handcuffs. The man, Mike, glared at the children with hate in his eyes. The woman was crying.

"That was smart of you to pull the distributer wire so the vehicle wouldn't start," said one of the policemen to the children.

Nick and Mandy stared at each other, open-mouthed.

"B-but we didn't," she sputtered.

"Well, *someone* did," said the officer. "These two were just sitting there in the truck, trying over and over to start it. We found the weapon under the seat."

If *we* didn't do it, who did? Mandy wondered. There was no one else out in the storm. Unless. . .

Nick had the same thought. "The old lighthouse keeper?" he whispered to her. "The *ghost*?"

Mandy looked dazed. "Stranger things have happened."

Chapter 19: The Secret Revealed

Mandy flopped down on her bed. The whole day seemed like a weird dream. Her head was swimming with images of black snakes, lightning bolts, spider webs, guns, and the kidnapper's ugly expression. How could all of that have happened in one day? She felt something underneath her and pulled out the old diary she had found in the attic. Could it have been just this morning? It seemed like a million years ago.

Mandy opened to the first page. *This book belongs to Dora Kimball* was written in faded graceful script. Kimball? Wow, Mandy thought, this must have belonged to the lighthouse keeper's wife. She shivered. What were the chances that she would find the book today, of all days?

As she skimmed through the pages, Mandy realized it was about the day-to-day happenings at the lighthouse—the weather, the garden, a visit from the lighthouse inspector, and the couple's two year old daughter.

November 1, 1899
Today Mary ran after a seagull on the shore, call-
ing "Kitty, Kitty," The gull is the same color as our cat
Samuel, white with gray and black markings. Imagine
her surprise when the 'kitty' spread its wings and lifted
into the sky. I could hardly wait to tell Isaiah. That lit-
tle girl is the apple of his eye. What joy she has brought
to our lives.

She turned to a fresh page. The writing changed, shaky and wandering.

Our dear Mary is ailing. She cries piteously and
eats little. I fear for her life.

The entries stopped after that. Mandy flipped through empty pages. There was one final entry at the end of the book.

December 12, 1899
How is it possible for one day to hold such terror and
such wonder? In the late afternoon, Isaiah came to me
to report a shipwreck on the ledge near Little Crumple.
Against my wishes, he set out in the skiff to give what
assistance he could. The conditions were daunting—high
wind and mountainous waves—but somehow he made

it to the schooner. I tended a fire on the beach so that he could find his way home.

After several hours in which I prayed continually, my husband washed up on the shore, clinging to a large bundle. He could not speak. In his eyes was a strange emptiness, as if he had witnessed a sight too horrible to bear. I hastened to bring him near the fire for warmth, but he would not let loose the bundle.

As I looked more closely, I could see it was two mattresses lashed together with pieces of lumber to keep it afloat. When I cut the rope, I found between the mattresses a box. To my utter amazement, inside was a baby girl, crying lustily. A small chest lay beside her. Later, I retrieved a key from my husband's pocket which opened the chest. It contained a silver locket and a message which read 'In great desperation and as a last hope I send my dear daughter Annie toward the light. I commend her into God's care.'

I gazed over the sea to the doomed vessel where an anguished mother had written this note. God had sent the baby to me to heal my heartbreak of losing my own little one. My dear husband made certain she would reach me.

I cannot, of course, tell others what has happened this day. I cannot risk that Annie will be taken from me. I will hide the note and locket and raise the baby as my own. The secret will die with me.

Mandy wiped tears from her cheeks. How sad for both mothers. Mrs. Kimball must have hidden the chest on the island later on. No one else had laid eyes on it...until today. "You were right, Papa Gene," Mandy whispered. "The answer to the mystery *was* on Little Crumple."

As she drifted off to sleep, she wondered if the restless spirits of the Captain and his wife had had a hand in all that had happened that day. Had Dora Kimball led Mandy to the packet on the island so that at last her secret could be known? Had the Captain helped them protect little Jonathan and prevented the kidnappers from escaping? Perhaps now they could rest in peace.

Chapter 20: Let Freedom Ring

Independence Day. How Mandy had dreaded this day. With Papa Gene gone, it couldn't possibly be the same. But so much had happened in the last few days that she almost felt like a different person.

The mystery solved. Little Jonathan reunited with his father. The kidnappers captured and in jail in Boston. And all because of her. . . and Nick. She glanced at her cousin. He clapped with the rest of the crowd as the high school band marched by playing America, the Beautiful. He had surprised her with his quick-thinking and bravery. He really wasn't so bad after all. He glanced her way and they shared a smile. She suddenly realized that her gawky, annoying cousin had become her friend.

The veterans filed past, rifles on their shoulders. Mandy's eyes filled with tears. Papa Gene should have been right there. Through the watery blur she thought she saw him—at the end of the row, looking right at her, a smile tugging at the corners of his mouth. She blinked. When she looked again, he was gone. "Thank you, Papa Gene," she whispered.

That afternoon at the family picnic, Mandy paused after the first bite of her mother's strawberry shortcake. "Mom," she said, raising her spoon for emphasis, "this is a little bit of heaven."

Mrs. Morrison looked startled for a moment. Then she smiled and said in a soft voice, "Thank you, Dear." Was that a tear she wiped from her own eye?

"Hey, Mandy, I have a present for you," Nick announced, placing a small box on the table beside her.

"A present for me? Why?" she asked. She untied the string and began to peel back the wrapping paper.

"It's kind of a late birthday present," he explained. "And. . . well, because you were so brave." His cheeks flushed pink.

Mandy lifted the lid. Underneath a layer of tissue paper nestled a sculpture, hand carved from a dark wood into coils. Two tiny red glass eyes glittered. A *snake?* She stared hard at Nick.

"Papa Gene carved it for me when I was nine," he said.

Mandy stared at him in astonishment. Sometimes she forgot that Papa Gene was Nick's grandfather, too. "You want to give it to *me*?" She turned it around and around in her hands, feeling the smoothness of the polished coils. Papa Gene's hands had touched this wood, carving it, shaping it with love in his heart. Love for Nick. How could Nick give it away?

"I thought you would like it," her cousin said. "A memento of our adventure." He grinned at her.

Mandy found herself grinning in return. "Gee, thanks. I'll *treasure* it always."

In the evening, everyone gathered at the waterfront for the fireworks. The colors exploded and sparkled, dancing high above the water.

A celebration of freedom, Mandy thought. She and Nick had freed Jonathan from the kidnappers. Papa Gene had fought in the war so that all of them could be free. She suddenly realized that her grandfather would always be with her. He lived on in her thoughts and memories. But he also lived on through her.

"Didn't I tell you it would be the best fireworks display Dyer Cove has ever seen?" Mrs. Morrison exclaimed, as the four of them headed toward the street.

"It was great, Mom," Mandy agreed.

Officer Bailey was directing traffic and he waved them over. "Good news, Miss Mandy. . . Nick. You're getting a reward."

"We are?" they both said at once. "How much?"

"Jonathan's father said you can pick it up at the bank tomorrow. Five thousand dollars."

Mandy's head was spinning. A reward? *Five thousand dollars?* So they had found a real "treasure" after all. They were rich. "Ya- hoo!" she yelled.

"Cool," said her cousin. "Now I can help out my family. Maybe I'll buy a pet python for myself. . . And I'd like one of those Seadog warm-up jackets. He thought for a moment. "And now," he said to Mandy, "you can come visit me in Nevada. Did I ever tell you about the old abandoned silver mine near my town?"

Mandy's eyes sparkled. "Haunted, right?"

Nick grinned. "Of course."

Author's Note

Dyer Point Light is a fictional lighthouse. However, the writing of *The Lightkeeper's Key* was inspired by real Maine lighthouse history and legends:

*Owls Head Light
The ghost of a former keeper roams the lighthouse, keeping the temperature turned down, polishing the brass, and trying to light the lantern in the tower. Keepers have found mysterious size 10 and ½ footprints on the walkway leading to the tower and the door unlocked (when they knew they had locked it!).

**Saddleback Ledge Light
In 1927 the keeper at this desolate lighthouse witnessed a strange event. Before the coming of a storm, seabirds attracted to the light crashed into the tower windows all night long. In the morning, the keeper found over a hundred birds dead or stunned on the catwalk and ground below. One

ten pound duck hurtled right into the lantern room and smashed into the Fresnel lens.

***Hendricks Head Light

One stormy winter night, a ship struck a ledge about a half mile away. The seas were too high for the lightkeeper to set out in his small boat, so he and his wife lit a bonfire on the beach to guide the shipwrecked crew. The crew climbed into the rigging to escape the raging sea, became covered with ice, and froze to death there. A woman on board put her baby daughter in a box tied between two mattresses and tossed her into the sea. The lightkeeper pulled the bundle from the pounding waves. Inside he found the baby and a note commending her into God's care. The keeper and his wife, who had just lost their baby daughter to illness, adopted the little girl and raised her as their own.

* *The Ghosts of New England Lighthouses* by William O. Thomson

** New England Lighthouses: A Virtual Tour by Jeremy D'Entremont

*** *The Lighthouses of New England* by Edward Rowe Snow

To find the treasure map and secret code,
visit: www.angeliperrow.com

Made in the USA
Charleston, SC
07 December 2009